Never Say A Mean Word Again

A Tale From
Medieval
Spain

written by

Jacqueline
Jules

illustrated by

Durga Yael
Bernhard

✦Wisdom Tales✦

Library of Congress Cataloging-in-Publication Data

Jules, Jacqueline, 1956-
  Never say a mean word again : a tale from Medieval Spain / written by Jacqueline Jules ;
illustrated by Durga Yael Bernhard.
    pages cm
  ISBN 978-1-937786-20-5 (hardcover : alk. paper) [1. Interpersonal relations--Fiction. 2. Justice--Fiction. 3. Fathers and sons--Fiction. 4. Spain--History--11th century--Fiction.]
    I. Bernhard, Durga, illustrator. II. Title.
      PZ7.J92947Nev 2014
      [E]--dc23
                                                                        2013044537

Production Date: January 2014
Plant & Location: Printed by Everbest Printing
(Guangzhou, China), Co. Ltd; Job / Batch: #118401

For information address Wisdom Tales,
P.O. Box 2682, Bloomington, Indiana 47402-2682

www.wisdomtalespress.com

To my granddaughter,
Willa Judith.
~ J. J.

For Meg & Warren.
~ D. Y. B.

Samuel, the son of the grand vizier, walked into the castle courtyard wearing a flowing purple robe.

His eyes were on the flowers and the fountains,
not where he was walking.

"OUCH!"
Too late. Samuel
bumped into Hamza,
the tax collector's son.
"You stepped on me!"
"Sorry," said Samuel.
"No, you're not! You
think you're better than
everybody else!"

Samuel's father,
the grand vizier,
was the most
powerful advisor
in the royal court.

Being the son of an important man didn't help Samuel make friends.

At the castle banquet, Samuel and Hamza were seated beside each other. Samuel felt uncomfortable. He didn't know if he should talk to Hamza or ignore him after what had happened in the courtyard.

He bit his lip and picked up his goblet.
It slipped out of his fingers.
Oh no! Water landed in Hamza's
plate, sloshing lamb sauce into
his lap. "I'm sorry," said
Samuel for the second
time in an hour.
"It was an
accident."

Hamza would not accept an apology. "DONKEY BRAIN! STUPID! LOOK WHAT YOU DID!" The brown stain in the middle of Hamza's white tunic looked like a mud puddle. Did it give him the right to call Samuel names?

Samuel's father didn't think so. "He spoke unkindly," remarked the vizier as Hamza rushed away.

"Will you punish him?" asked Samuel hopefully.

The vizier rubbed his chin. "No. You will take care of this matter."

"Me?"

"Yes," confirmed the vizier. "Make sure Hamza never says a mean word to you again."

No one ignored the vizier. He was considered the wisest man in the kingdom.

"I will," promised Samuel.

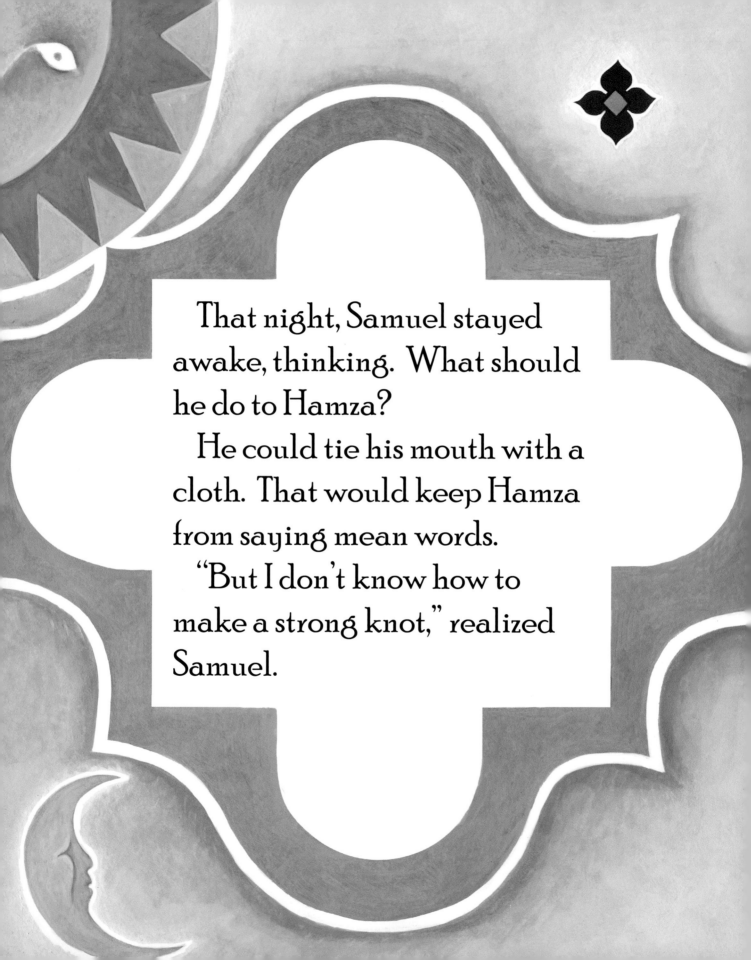

That night, Samuel stayed awake, thinking. What should he do to Hamza?

He could tie his mouth with a cloth. That would keep Hamza from saying mean words.

"But I don't know how to make a strong knot," realized Samuel.

Maybe
he could train a
monkey to sit on
Hamza's
shoulders. The monkey
could clamp Hamza's lips shut.
Training a monkey would
take time.
And where
would he get a
monkey?

What about lemons? He could make Hamza eat one. That would be a good punishment for a boy who said mean things.

"My father will be proud," thought Samuel.

The next morning, Samuel knocked on Hamza's door with a large lemon in his hand.

"Lemon juice won't clean the stain," Hamza said. "My mother already tried it."

Samuel hadn't come to clean Hamza's clothes!
What should he say now?
"That lemon is the size of a ball." Hamza laughed.
Hamza's comment gave Samuel an idea
for a challenge. "I bet you can't catch it."
"I bet I can." Hamza stepped outside.
They threw the lemon back and
forth until it was so battered,
it couldn't have made
anyone's mouth
pucker.

The next day, Samuel had a better plan than a lemon. He walked to Hamza's house with ink and paper. He would make Hamza write out a promise, a promise he could show the vizier.

But when Hamza opened his door, he didn't wait to hear what Samuel wanted.

"Paper! I love to draw!"

Together, they drew a picture of the castle on the hill.

Samuel went home that day, worried. Everyone was expected to obey the vizier, especially his own son.

"What if my father asks about Hamza?" wondered Samuel.

Samuel went to Hamza's house the next day and the next. He tried beating Hamza at chess. It was a tie.

He tried a water fight at the lake. They laughed too much.

Soon, they became used to seeing each other every day.

One sunny afternoon, the vizier found them in the courtyard playing.

Hamza put four marbles in Samuel's hand.

"These are for you, my friend," he said.

The vizier stared at the boys. "What is going on here?" Samuel gulped, worried his father would be disappointed in him.

Then he remembered
what the vizier had said
at the banquet.
"Make sure Hamza never says
a mean word to you again."
"My friend just gave me a
gift," Samuel explained.
The vizier tilted his head.
"Then you did what I asked?"
Samuel looked at
Hamza's smiling face.
"Yes, Father. I did."

The End

AUTHOR'S NOTE

This story was inspired by a medieval legend about the Jewish poet Samuel Ha-Nagid, who was the vizier (highest royal advisor) in Muslim Granada, a city in Spain. According to the legend, the caliph (or king) ordered that a man be severely punished for cursing the vizier. Later, when the caliph saw Samuel joking with the man, Samuel explained by saying, "I have torn out his angry tongue and given him a kind one instead." This powerful example of making a friend of one's enemy appears in several sources. I saw it first in *Pentateuch & Haftorahs*, edited by Dr. J. H. Hertz. A version in the JewishEncylopedia.com says that Samuel made friends with his enemy by giving him a gift.

As vizier, Samuel Ha-Nagid was the commander of a Muslim army, an unusual position for a Jewish man. Equally remarkable is the story of how Samuel came to the royal court in the first place. He was originally the owner of a spice shop. On the side, he wrote letters for a servant in the court. His writing attracted the attention of the vizier at the time, who then employed Samuel's skills at the palace. From there, Samuel rose to power. Thus, Samuel's success at court came from his exceptional writing ability. In addition to being a statesman, Samuel was known as a gifted poet and scholar.

Everything we know about Samuel Ha-Nagid depicts his life as an adult. In *Never Say a Mean Word Again*, I imagined the story as if it took place between his son and a Muslim child at court. By changing the ages of the main characters, I changed most of the details, only retaining the essence of the tale in the process.

The Spain of Samuel Ha-Nagid's time was unique in its cultural and religious richness. Muslim armies had crossed into Spain and Portugal from North Africa in 711 CE, where they remained for almost eight hundred years, influencing many aspects of the culture. Because Europeans called people from that part of Africa "Moors," the area of Spain that Muslims dominated is sometimes called "Moorish Spain," but it is also called Al-Andalus by many scholars. At the height of their power, the Muslim caliphs controlled most of what is now Spain and Portugal, but by the time of Queen Isabella and King Ferdinand, they only held small areas such as Granada. For many centuries, the areas that were ruled by Muslims often were noteworthy for the degree to which Muslims, Jews, and Christians exchanged cultural ideas, promoted tolerance, and lived in peace. The story of *Never Say a Mean Word Again* is set during those times, which some refer to as "The Golden Age of Spain."

JACQUELINE JULES is a former school librarian and
teacher, and the author of over two dozen books for children,
including the award-winning Zapato Power series. Many of her
titles are of special interest to young Jewish readers, including
The Hardest Word, a National Jewish Book Award finalist,
and Sydney Taylor Honor Award winners *Sarah Laughs* and
Benjamin and the Silver Goblet. Jacqueline's sensitivity to
themes that engage children is evident in her choice of topics,
such as being away at camp, starting at a new school and being
unable to communicate in English, name calling, and being
from a different culture in America. She lives with her family
in Northern Virginia, near Washington, D.C. Visit her online at
www.jacquelinejules.com.

DURGA YAEL BERNHARD was raised in New York's
Hudson Valley and began painting at the age of thirteen. Ms.
Bernhard is the illustrator, designer, and author of numerous
award-winning children's books, including fiction and non-fiction,
multicultural folktales, and concept books. She brings a variety
of interests to her work, including a strong grounding in African
music and dance; studies in Eastern and Western religion; and
a love of nature that fills her daily life in the Catskill Mountain
wilderness where she makes her home. Ms. Bernhard is also a
fine art painter and a children's teacher of Hebrew, Judaics, and
art. Visit her blog and website at dyaelbernhard.com.